Kimara Crossing

David R. Beshears

Book two in the series following
Jim, future Prince of the Frontier Worlds

Greybeard Publishing
Washington State

Greybeard Publishing
P.O. Box 480
McCleary, WA 98557-0480

ISBN 978-1-947231-08-5

Kimara Crossing

Chapter One

The sixty-foot sloop glided across the smooth surface of the inland sea. The wooden sailboat, with its single mast and jib under full canvas, had departed from the north shore port two days earlier and was now a day and a half out from Port Kimara on the south coast. The morning Kimaran sun splayed sparkling light across the water.

Two of the ship's crew were working the sails, another helmed the wheel; five others of the crew were in the ship's mess below deck.

Jim was standing at the rail, looking out across the water. He listened to the wind in the sails, the creaking of the rigging. He had made this trip a number of times over the previous two years, journeying from the Academy to the Capital every four months between training sessions. He would spend two weeks with his family at the governor's estate and then return to the school for the next session.

Jim was fifteen years old. He had been on Kimara a little over two years, since his father had been named Governor of Kimara, the capitol world of the Frontier Worlds. He was dressed in brown leather trousers and a matching open vest over a tan shirt, and had taken to wearing his brown hair shoulder length in the style of the native population.

Wyatt and Victor came up on deck and walked over to stand beside him at the rail.

"Rather pungent flavor, but definitely filling," said Wyatt. Jim's friend was human, sixteen years old and a native of Kimara. He was dressed in dark trousers and jacket, wore his shoulder-length hair pulled back and tied in a short, three inch ponytail. A knife was sheathed in his high boots, and he kept a hand sling ready at his belt.

"I always enjoy the ship's breakfast," said Victor. He was a TholMahr, a humanoid native of a nearby planet called Mahrahn. His gold eyes held cats-eye pupils, were shaded behind round, amber-colored glasses. He had a thin face, white wispy hair with long braids extending from his temples. He had a sinewy frame, strong, rope-thin muscles. His movements were smooth and agile. He was dressed all in black, including thin black gloves covering extraordinarily long fingers. He kept a pair of short wooden staffs sheathed on his back.

His true TholMahr name was "Lanahorvictahrahntock", but as this was nearly unpronounceable by humans he went by Victor. He had been Jim's companion and protector almost since Jim first arrived on Kimara.

"Me too, Victor," said Jim. The sloop was the Governor's yacht, and Jim's father made sure the crew was treated well. Jim ate better on board ship than he did at the Academy. "Quite tasty."

"I'm not complaining," said Wyatt. "It's just a bit spicy for my taste... for breakfast."

"And for lunch?" Jim asked, already knowing the answer.

Wyatt took a long breath and grinned. "Looking forward to it," he said.

The ship's captain came up on deck then and worked his way aft. He took the ladder up to the quarterdeck, gave a nod to his helmsman as he took his position to one side of the wheel. Captain Bellamy was tall, broad shouldered, neat and clean-cut. He wore his hair pulled back tight and bound in a long ponytail.

The sloop was the governor's in name only. For all practical purposes, the ship belonged to the Captain.

A crewman rushed past Jim and quickly took the ladder up to the quarterdeck. He said something to the captain and the two of them stepped over to the rail. The captain brought a pair of binoculars out from a compartment and used them to study the horizon.

Jim and his friends looked out across the water, trying to see what the captain was looking at.

"Do you see anything?" asked Wyatt.

"No," said Jim. "Nothing."

After a few moments, Victor gave a sharp nod to the horizon. "There," he stated.

Jim and Wyatt struggled to see it, still saw nothing.

And then... *there.*

Jim saw something... a silhouette sitting low on the horizon. It grew as he watched, narrowed then as it tacked and looked to come directly toward them, bow on.

"A ship."

"It approaches," said Victor.

Jim nodded, turned and looked up at Captain Bellamy. The captain lowered his binoculars. He maintained his sure, steady manner, but Jim could see that he was troubled. He didn't like what he was seeing.

He said something to the crewman waiting beside him. The man brought up a handset and spoke into it. Moments later, the others of the ship's crew came up from below deck and began moving into position on the main deck. All were Kimaran natives, descended from the original human colonists. Several were carrying stun rods, others were armed with short swords or bludgeons.

A young crewman moved up to stand at the rail beside Jim and looked to the growing silhouette. Johann was a friend of Jim's, the two having first becoming acquainted at the Academy, then continuing their friendship after Johann had been assigned to the governor's yacht.

"Who are they, Johann?" asked Jim.

"We're not sure," said Johann. "Systems haven't identified the ship as yet, and they're not responding to our hails."

"It's Guild," Wyatt stated, as if fact.

"Another few hundred yards, and we will know that for sure," said Johann. The ship's monitoring systems would be able to identify the exact ship as soon as it came into range.

The crewman on the quarterdeck picked up the handset and held the receiver to his ear. A moment later he spoke to the captain.

Captain Bellamy looked down to the main deck, looked to Johann. He waved a hand toward the hatch. Johann nodded and turned to Jim.

"This way, Jim," he said, moving away from the rail.

"What is it?"

"We can't have you a target."

"Come, Jim." Victor had already taken a step toward the hatch, following Johann.

"It's Guild, isn't it?" Wyatt asked Johann.

"It is." Johann guided Jim and the others across the deck.

There could be only one reason for a Guild ship to approach the Governor's yacht en route from the Academy to the Port Kimara.

They were after Jim, the son of the governor.

Wyatt led the way through the hatch and down into the hold. Jim followed, and Victor after. Johann closed the hatch behind them, remaining above deck with the rest of the crew.

They took the narrow hall past several doors and entered the main hold. Victor closed and locked the door behind them.

The center of the room was clear, with tables and chairs scattered about to either side, counters and cabinets along the walls. Victor and Wyatt stepped into the middle of the room as Jim moved to the nearest table and sat on the corner.

"I don't like this," he said. "We should be up there with the others."

"Not so," said Victor. He brought his pair of short staff weapons out of their sheaths, flipped them about using his long fingers. "At the moment, you can best serve the crew by remaining here."

"He's right, Jim," said Wyatt. "Up there, you would only divide the crew's attention. They can't be looking after you and defending the ship at the same time."

"I don't need babysitting."

"That is not the issue," said Wyatt. "You are the son of the governor. This is the governor's yacht. They are the ship's crew. Let them do their job."

"And we shall do ours," said Victor. He held the pair of staffs at the ready.

Wyatt grinned. "You, maybe. I'm just here for the ride."

"Of course." Victor knew that if anyone came through that door, Wyatt would be standing right beside him. They would do whatever it took to protect the governor's son.

"Why now?" asked Jim. He folded his arms across his chest.

"Why now what?" asked Wyatt.

"Why is the Guild taking such an interest in me now?"

The Founders Guild had made only a handful of attempts at grabbing Jim in the past, and nothing for many months. And since the Guild had no reason to grab Jim that he could think of, then they had to be making this attempt for someone else.

The pirates...

They heard raised voices then coming from above decks, the sound muffled as it came through the timbers of the ship. Jim couldn't make out the words, but they didn't sound panicked just yet.

He pushed off the table and stood beside Victor. Wyatt moved up beside his friends. Together they faced the door, but their attention was focused above them, beyond the ceiling to above decks.

The raised voices grew louder, more aggressive, occasionally accompanied by angry cries.

They heard scuffling then, as of boots scraping on deck boards; the sounds of fighting.

The sounds of fighting moved below decks and into the hallway beyond the door. At that, Victor moved half a step ahead of the others and readied himself.

The enclosed space made Wyatt's hand sling of no use; he pulled his knife from the boot sheath.

Jim prepared himself for hand-to-hand, as was part of his training.

There came the sounds of scuffling and fighting from just beyond the locked door, accompanied by loud grunts and several groans. This lasted for maybe half a minute.

And then... the sounds beyond the door stopped; No voices, no scuffling of feet.

The sounds of the fighting above deck began to fade, diminished over a half minute, a minute... faded finally to silence.

Another three minutes passed, then three minutes more. All was quiet. There were no voices; there were no footsteps.

Nothing.

"Well?" Wyatt asked, hardly above a whisper. He slipped his knife back into the boot sheath.

"I do not know," said Victor. He chose not to sheath his staff weapons just yet. "I believe we wait."

"Yeah... no." Wyatt exhaled tiredly. "I don't think anybody's coming."

"We gotta go see what's what," said Jim.

Victor served as protector to the son of the governor, but Jim was not obligated to take orders. This sometimes added complexity to his responsibility.

And being Jim's friend only added additional complications.

"Very well," he said, grudgingly. He started toward the door, looking back briefly at Jim. His expression could not be misinterpreted... *you will stay behind me.*

Jim gave him a thumbs-up. Victor unlocked the door, hesitated, then opened it. The hallway beyond was empty. There was no sign there had been a conflict.

They worked their way forward, stopping at the first door in the passage. Pushing the door open, Victor looked into the communications room. It was small, just large enough to hold a counter and chair, comm equipment mounted on the wall above the counter. The equipment had been damaged, clearly beyond repair.

Victor looked back to Jim and Wyatt; he shook his head and continued forward, up and out of the hold, onto the deck.

Jim moved past and around Victor.

"Uhhh..." He moved slowly across the deck. "Where is everybody?"

There was no answer to that. They saw some signs of there having been a skirmish, including damaged railing, scuffs and scratches on the deck, cut lines and more. Continuing to search about the deck, they found several splatters of blood, though nothing major.

But there were no people; there was no sign of crew, no sign of guildsmen.

"Where's the ship?" asked Wyatt, standing at the rail.

Jim and Victor came up beside him. There was no Guild ship.

"Okay, this is just odd," said Jim.

Victor looked out across the water, looked all the way to the horizon. Seeing nothing, he turned away from the rail, leaving Jim and Wyatt.

"What do you think, Wyatt?" asked Jim.

"I think our crew chased the Guild back to their ship and followed after 'em."

"Okay... okay, I can see that. Then what?"

"Heck if I know," said Wyatt.

"Over here, please," said Victor. He was standing at the starboard rail. He waited until Jim and Wyatt joined him there. The inland sea's south shore was no more than half a mile distant. As they watched, it appeared they were drifting parallel to the shore, not closing any nearer.

"Any sign of the crew?" asked Wyatt.

"I do not believe they went ashore." stated Victor. "We must decide our next course of action."

Jim leaned forward, rested his arms on the rail. He looked fore and aft. The jib and mainsail were luffing. The ship was drifting with the current.

Victor wanted a course of action...

"Are you suggesting we go ashore?" he asked.

Victor clasped his hands together and continued looking across to the shore. He considered his response.

"We do not know what has happened to the ship's crew, and we have no reason to believe the Guild will not return. Should they return, I doubt that we would be able prevent them from taking you."

"So, we go ashore."

Victor nodded. "And allow the ship to continue to drift after our disembarkation, thereby making it difficult for them to determine where we went ashore."

"All right," said Wyatt. "You two gather supplies, I'll prep the dinghy."

Victor looked to Jim, who slowly pushed off the rail. Jim looked from Wyatt to Victor.

"Right. Let's do it."

Chapter Two

Wyatt hopped out of the wooden dinghy as the hull of the small craft slid aground in the shallow surf. He pulled the boat the rest of the way ashore as Jim and Victor quickly jumped out and pushed.

With the dinghy beached, Wyatt began looking for a place to hide it. Victor unloaded the supplies and Jim stood looking offshore.

The governor's yacht was nearly out of sight.

"Father won't be happy," he said, speaking over his shoulder. "I lost his ship."

Victor had been with Jim long enough to read the young human's sense of humor, though he often had difficulty returning it.

"It shall be recovered," he stated flatly.

"I'm sure it will." Jim turned back to the beach.

Victor had finished unloading the supplies and Wyatt was dragging the empty dinghy to a cluster of brush that grew at the base of a tall cliff. The beach itself was little more than a narrow band of sand between the water and the bluff.

Jim knelt down next to the supplies. They had packed cheese, salami, bread and packaged foodstuff into a canvas bag; clothing, emergency supplies, mess supplies they packed into two knapsacks. Two leather water skins and a few other odds and ends had been tossed into the dinghy at the last minute. These he began stuffing into the knapsacks.

Victor stood beside him and looked up the beach. Jim glanced up at him as he finished packing.

"Looks like we've a long way to go, eh Victor?" he asked.

"I do not know precisely where we are, but yes; a long way to go."

Wyatt returned from hiding the dinghy. "We could wait for Captain Bellamy to find us; or the governor."

"I don't think so," said Jim. "Wyatt, we don't know what happened to the captain. And my father doesn't know to look for us. Not yet."

Victor reached down and picked up one of the knapsacks. He hooked one of the water skins onto his belt. "In any case, neither would know where to look for us any more than do the guildsmen."

Jim got to his feet, grabbed the second knapsack and water skin. He looked up the beach. The sand eventually gave way to trees and brush, the cliff continuing as far as he could see.

Wyatt picked up the canvas bag and the three started walking. After twenty yards, Victor pointed out tiny animal tracks in the sand beginning at the waterline and ending at the base of the cliff. Wyatt recognized these as Thrum tracks. Thrums were finger-sized, multi-legged creatures with short claws and sharp teeth.

The three reached the trees and quickly found themselves walking into and out of shadows. The tree trunks were thin and smooth, branching high to the overhead canopy, which was sparsely leaved. The sandy soil beneath their feet was light colored. The bushes, growing in clusters along the base of the cliff, had broad, flat leaves and bright berries. Wyatt said that the berries would be edible once ripe, which they weren't.

They passed into and out of several open beaches over the next two hours. They were looking for a way to leave the shore and head inland, but as yet were blocked by the cliffs. None were eager to attempt the climb, and they felt they had time to continue searching for a safe passage.

They entered another grove of trees near dusk, worked their way over to the cliff wall and followed it until they found a cave-like recess in the base. Here is where they would spend the night.

Once settled in, they shared a meal of cheese, bread, and a package of mixed nuts and berries. They decided it would be safer not to make a campfire. Fortunately, this time of year on Kimara the night would be warm.

After their light dinner, Jim watched Wyatt practice with his hand sling as Victor explored their surroundings before dark.

Wyatt hung the canvas bag on a tree trunk to use as a target. Hooking the finger loop at the end of one cord of his sling onto a finger, he held the knot at the end of the other cord in his palm. The pocket now hanging free, he loaded a walnut sized stone.

He held his hand out a moment and let the weight of the stone register in his mind. He moved his hand slowly from side to side, once, twice, three times. He quickly spun the sling... and let it go.

The stone hit the target dead center.

Wyatt had been using a hand sling for as long as he could remember. He had learned from his father. His father had learned from Wyatt's grandmother.

Hand slings had come to Kimara with the first colonists from old Earth, were used first as sport, occasionally as a hunting weapon.

He missed his second shot, barely, and made the next two.

Victor returned from his brief explore, careful to avoid Wyatt's line of fire.

"How's it look, Victor?" asked Jim.

"The grove continues for another hundred paces; I did not enter the beach beyond. From what I could see, it extends for a considerable distance. The grove itself is clear of immediate danger."

"Sounds good," said Jim.

"The grove here is deep. We are a hundred and eighty paces from the shoreline."

Despite Victor's words of assurance, Jim knew that his friend and protector would get little sleep. Nothing that Jim might say would change that. Still, he would do what he could.

"We'll take turns standing watch," he said. "I'll take first, Wyatt second. Victor, you take third."

"As you say," said Victor.

Wyatt let loose another stone with his sling. It hit the target.

"Sure," he said. He walked to the target to retrieve his weapon stones from the ground at the base of the tree. As he approached, he sensed movement above them. He lifted his gaze.

Three large birds were circling high overhead, their silhouettes black against the gray sky.

Starbirds.

Wyatt knew they would soon be going after the Thrums that had come out of the surf and were now feeding on the cliff walls.

Chapter Three

In the morning they shared a package of dried fruit and a small wedge of cheese. With breakfast out of the way, they gathered up their gear and started out, continuing their journey east along the coast. They quickly came out of the grove of trees and started along the open beach.

It was a long stretch of sand, as Victor had said it would be. The cliff wall was in morning shadow, the Kimaran sun rising from behind the bluff. They occasionally saw darker shadows scurrying about the cracks and crevices of the cliff. At one point Wyatt pointed out a larger, six-legged animal that was chasing after one of the smaller creatures. Its clawed feet gripped the jagged rocky wall while its hands grasped after its prey.

While Jim and Wyatt focused their attention on the cliffs for signs of a way up and so inland, Victor watched the sea. His vision was much keener than theirs, and he would be the first to spot a ship on the water.

They reached the next grove of trees in midmorning, entered and soon lost sight of the sea. They continued under the safety of the canopy for several hundred yards before stopping for their first break of the day. Wyatt sorted through the packages in the canvas bag, finally chose mixed nuts as a snack. They washed it down with a few swallows of water.

Their water supply was good for now, but they would need to find a new source within the next few days.

Starting out again, they worked their way to the base of the cliff and followed it east. The sun appeared overhead near midday and its rays streamed in through the canopy and reached the grove floor. They stopped for lunch, started again after only a few minutes, eager to continue.

Reaching the perimeter of the grove, they moved out onto the next stretch of beach. It was only forty yards wide and a few dozen feet deep. Starting across the sand, they noticed a dark, straight line in the distance, starting at the base of the cliff and ending at the water's edge.

"What is that?" asked Wyatt, more to himself than to his companions.

They approached it, whatever *it* was...

It was a trench, three feet wide, two feet deep, and lined with square clay tiles. It ran from the cliff to the surf. Looking back to the cliff, they saw the trench began at the base of an open-face gutter sloping down from a storm drain access about two-thirds up the cliff. This gutter was made of the same clay tiles that lined the trench.

"It's old," said Victor.

"Ancient." Jim knelt down beside the trench and studied the siding. Many of the square tiles were broken, the cracks wide and in some cases with weeds growing from them. The clay was discolored from many decades of exposure to the Kimara weather.

Wyatt, standing beside Jim, was looking up the cliff wall, his eyes following the down-gutter. The slope was steep, but gentle enough that runoff coming from the storm drain could flow easily down to the trench.

"We can do that," he said. "No problem."

Jim and Victor followed Wyatt's gaze up the gutter to the dark opening of the storm drain. Climbing the gutter was possible. The grade was moderate enough, and there were enough handholds.

Then what?

"You want us to go into the storm drains?" asked Jim. The drain opening looked tall enough, only just, but it wasn't going to be all that comfortable.

"It goes somewhere," said Wyatt. "Wherever that *somewhere* is, it'll be up top."

"That it will," said Victor.

"Any thoughts on where that might be?" asked Jim.

"Not at this time." Victor looked from Jim to Wyatt, again to the sloping down-gutter. He started toward it then, walking alongside the trench, leaving his friends to follow him.

Reaching the gutter, he stepped into the trench and started climbing. The slope wasn't as gentle as he would have liked, but it was enough. Cracked and broken clay tiles provided handholds and footholds, though they weren't always in the best of locations.

Jim followed Victor and Wyatt followed Jim. While the others carried their knapsacks on their backs, Wyatt had to tie the canvas bag that he was carrying to his belt in order to free up both hands. This made climbing rather awkward.

"I am not liking this," he said.

"Wasn't this your idea?" asked Jim.

"The decision was a collective effort."

Victor, meanwhile, said nothing. He climbed. Those below him continued their good-natured exchange, something Victor had long ago grown accustomed to and now considered little more than background noise. They seemed to enjoy the back and forth. He had in the past made attempts at joining in on their exchanges, but these had always come across as clumsy efforts and he had never been comfortable in those attempts.

Approaching the top of the down-gutter, Victor had to reach over a broken lip of smooth clay panels in order to pull himself up and onto the small landing. He found himself facing a storm drain barely four feet tall, three feet wide.

Their journey through the drains would be uncomfortable at best.

Victor turned around and looked outward... the inland sea stretched far to the horizon where water met sky.

Movement then caught his attention. He kept his head still and shifted his eyes left.

About a quarter of a mile offshore... a ship was traveling slow, paralleling the coast. It was as yet far to their left, and it would be a while before it passed before them, but they were already in visual range.

Victor hoped their focus was on the beach and not high up the cliff wall.

"Quickly, please," he said calmly. There was no urgency in his tone, but the point was clear.

Jim picked up the pace.

"Company?" asked Wyatt, below Jim.

"Company," stated Victor.

Jim reached the landing; he and Victor backed into the shadow of the storm drain, both squatting to squeeze inside. They watched the ship as it approached. It had a mast, but at the moment the sail was furled and the ship was under power. This allowed it much more control.

"Wyatt," Jim mumbled. "You might want to pick it up."

"I'm coming, I'm coming." He was in fact already scrambling up onto the landing.

Jim scooted aside and Wyatt moved passed him and went into the storm drain. Jim backed in further then and knelt again, continuing to watch the ship.

The configuration of the craft was unfamiliar. It wasn't one of the governor's fleet.

The ship slowly passed just offshore. Only when Jim was sure that it wasn't stopping did he back fully into the drain. He asked Victor to turn around so that he could get into his friend's knapsack. He rummaged about and pulled out the hand lantern. He turned the crank half a dozen times, locked it in place and turned it on.

Jim worked his way past the others and led the way, holding the lantern out in front of him. The shimmering light pushed out ahead of them. Behind them, the rectangle of light of the drain opening grew smaller and smaller until it disappeared altogether.

They walked hunched over, leg muscles straining, the tops of their heads occasionally striking the ceiling. They stopped after several minutes to ease their stiffening muscles.

Jim gave the hand lantern another half dozen cranks, sat it on the floor between them. The hazy sphere of light reached just past them into the tunnel. From the dark came an empty, hollow silence. The only sounds were from their breathing and the occasional shuffling of their feet as they struggled to get comfortable.

They started again without comment, Jim continuing to lead the way. After another hundred feet, they came to a side-shaft emptying into the mainline they were traveling through. The shaft opening was in the wall on their left, a foot above the floor. It was two feet tall and two feet wide.

They continued past.

Another minute and Jim stopped and knelt down.

"Heads up," he said.

Victor and Wyatt stopped behind him.

"What is it?" asked Wyatt.

"I'm not sure." There was something different about the darkness ahead. It was less black, less dark. Jim turned off the lantern. They waited.

It took a few moments for their eyes to adjust.

"I see," said Victor, looking past Jim.

There was light up ahead; it was faint, but definitely light. Jim kept the lantern turned off as they started forward again, albeit more slowly.

The light came from a shaft in the tunnel ceiling, the luminosity spilling down to the main drain line from an iron grate twelve feet above. A rusty, rickety set of ladder rungs were bolted to the side of the storm drain and up into the shaft.

"It doesn't look very safe," said Wyatt.

Jim handed the lantern to Victor and rested a hand on one of the rungs.

Victor turned on the lantern and held it nearer the ladder. The bolts that held the rungs to the wall were rusted; some were missing.

"I agree with Wyatt," he said. "Please use caution, Jim."

"Right. Here goes." Jim set a foot on one of the lower rungs, tested it, put his weight on it. It held. He tested the rung he was holding onto. It also held.

He worked his way up into the shaft. Most of the rungs were loose, but all held his weight. When he reached the top he pushed at the grate.

It showed no signs of giving way.

He stared up through the grate. The sky overhead was bright blue.

He shifted his position on the ladder, set his back against the shaft wall, and pushed hard; still nothing. He tried different positions, different angles.

Nothing.

Wyatt called up from below. "What's the holdup there, Jim?"

"I'm coming down." Jim worked his way back down, several of the rungs threatening to come free. Victor and Wyatt moved aside as he reached them and stepped off the bottom rung.

"So?" asked Wyatt.

"Sealed shut, maybe rusted shut. Whichever, we're not getting out that way."

Wyatt looked longingly up into the shaft. Jim grinned and shook his head. He knew that Wyatt was considering climbing up the shaft himself and giving the grate a try.

Victor didn't give him the opportunity.

"Come," he stated firmly. He started down the tunnel, taking his turn in the lead, lantern in hand.

Half a minute further and they came to another side-shaft, this one much like the first, about two feet tall and two feet wide.

There was one difference.

"Do you smell that?" asked Wyatt.

A strong musty smell, an animal smell, was pushing out from the side-shaft.

"Of course I do," said Victor. He had in fact picked up the smell some way back. He peered into the dark of the shaft. "It is a nest."

Jim warily eyed the side-shaft opening.

Oh, boy...

"I have a question," whispered Wyatt. When no one prompted him, he simply asked. "What do they eat? Down here?"

"Thanks for that, Wyatt," said Jim. To Victor then, "What say we move along?"

"Of course," Victor repeated, started walking again.

Wyatt followed at his heels. "Pick it up, Victor."

Victor said nothing, but the others noted they were traveling just a tad faster; about as fast as they were able while walking hunched over in a four-foot high tunnel.

A few dozen awkward strides and Jim began hearing something... or thought he heard something: scraping, as of claws on hard clay tiles.

My imagination?

The sound was coming from behind him, and it was coming nearer.

Not my imagination...

It was more than scraping now: animal snorts, guttural.

Victor must have heard it too, with his keener sense of hearing, because they were moving even faster, if that was possible. Jim's strides stretched out, his head continually bumping against the ceiling. He could hear the breathing of the animal directly behind him. He dared not look back, as doing so would slow him down; or perhaps worse, he might trip and fall.

Up ahead, Victor was suddenly bathed in natural light; his body rose up and disappeared.

Another up-shaft, thought Jim.

The guttural snorts behind him were nearer yet. He felt something strike at his heel. He stopped suddenly then when ahead of him Wyatt stopped and leapt up onto the metal rungs of the ladder. The animal ran headlong into Jim, its snout striking him in the back of his legs.

From up in the shaft came the sound of a rung ripping from the shaft wall, but it didn't seem to slow Wyatt down at all. His feet disappeared from Jim's view.

Jim struck out behind him with his foot, felt his boot strike something. He reached up into the shaft and blindly grabbed at a rung. It was loose and threatened to come free, but held when he pulled himself up. Above him, Wyatt stopped his climb as Victor above him worked at the grate. Jim had to stop and wait, his feet only two rungs off the mainline floor. He continued to kick at the animal as the creature clawed and bit at him.

Victor must have managed to push up the grate, because Wyatt began climbing again. Jim followed, agonizingly slow, one rung and then another. The creature continued to tug at his boots.

Jim grasped the top rung, the light of the outside washing over him. Victor and Wyatt grasped at his arms and pulled him up out of the shaft. He was tossed to one side as Victor dropped the grate back into place.

Jim shifted about and sat up. Wyatt gave him a pat on the shoulder, stepped over and picked up the hand lantern that had been thrown aside. He leaned over the grate and held the lantern above it.

"Geez," he mumbled.

Jim moved over beside Wyatt. Victor stood opposite.

Long, gray-haired fingers grasped at the grate; thick fingers with dirty black claws. In the shaft below, Jim could see black eyes set to either side of a long, wet snout. Gray lips were pulled back, exposing yellow teeth.

"Cute fella." Jim straightened and turned away from the storm drain. He looked for the first time at their surroundings.

They were in the middle of a small, weedy field of dry, yellow grass. A hundred yards to the south was a cluster of dilapidated, single-storey buildings. They looked at first glance to be abandoned.

Wyatt stood beside Jim.

"Take a look at your boots, my friend."

Chapter Four

There were long, deep claw marks all up and down the upper parts of Jim's boots, some deep enough that he could see his leather trousers tucked inside. There were deep teeth marks on the ankles and heels of both boots.

Jim considered himself lucky. A few seconds more and the creature would have shredded its way completely through his boots and who knew what would have happened.

Victor was looking at Jim with some concern.

"I'm good," Jim assured him. He looked up. "So where are we?"

"Let's go find out," said Wyatt. They started across the field toward the building complex. The field and complex were surrounded on all sides by a forest of tall, blue-green trees.

There looked to be a central building with a number of offshoot wings, some long and narrow, some wide and much shorter; some had windows, others solid walls. From all indications, the complex was long abandoned. The buildings were decrepit, gutters hanging loose, windows broken, in some cases roofs sagging.

They worked their way toward the central building, following a walkway between two wings to a set of double doors. A worn, faded sign was mounted on the wall above the doors: "Academy of Kimara".

"The original academy," said Wyatt.

Jim looked questioningly at Wyatt. *Original?*

"It was established not long after we colonized Kimara; they closed it down maybe a hundred years ago when the new academy was built."

"Then... you know where we are," said Jim.

"I know where we are. But that doesn't mean I know how to get from here to the estate."

"I see," said Victor.

"I don't," said Jim.

"Everyone knows of the original academy," said Wyatt. "But I never knew where it was located."

Great... thought Jim, but he said nothing. They reached the doors and Victor pulled one open. It resisted at first, creaked and shuddered on its hinges.

Entering, they found themselves in a front foyer. The walls were bare. Light shone through a pair of filthy windows. Wyatt gave the hand lantern several cranks and turned it on.

The floor was caked in a layer of dust. Open doors on the left and the right led to small offices. They continued across the foyer and entered a wide hallway running left and right into two of the academy's wings. In the wall directly opposite was another set of doors. Opening these, they saw another foyer with doors leading to still more wings.

They stepped back into the main hallway and over the next hour wandered the halls and rooms of the ancient academy, always on the lookout for something, anything, that might help them with their journey home. There were classrooms, training facilities, dormitories, offices, supply and utility rooms. Most were empty. Most of what little remained had deteriorated over the decades.

Working their way along a narrow secondary hallway with no windows, they found a small room with communication equipment on a counter and mounted on the walls.

Wyatt set the hand lantern on a counter as Jim slid into a rickety metal chair and scooted forward. He began looking closely at several pieces of equipment, absently flipping one switch and another.

"What'd you say before, Wyatt? A hundred years?"

"That's what I said."

"That looks about right." Jim had read of such ancient communications equipment in his academic studies. "There hasn't been anything like this in decades, at least."

"I would imagine the world has changed much since those early days," said Victor.

"My ancestors brought Old Earth with them," said Wyatt, shrugging. "It took a couple of generations before they could call themselves Kimaran."

That made sense to Jim. "I can understand that," he said.

"We adapted to Kimara much more than Kimara adapted to us." Wyatt looked across at Victor. "But yes, technology has changed since those early days; it advanced in some cases, simply changed directions in others; whatever Kimara required."

Jim leaned back in the rusty chair and folded his arms across his chest.

"And yet we still can't call home," he said.

"Perhaps we should continue," said Victor.

Jim slid the chair back and stood up. "Right. The day isn't getting any younger."

They worked their way back to the main hallway and followed this to another hall that took them toward the rear of the complex. They eventually found themselves in a smaller, secondary foyer.

Victor walked over to the glass double doors. Several panels were broken, and those that weren't were coated with years of grime. The left door scraped across the floor when he pushed it open.

Jim and Wyatt went to a large map that was mounted on one wall, set behind glass. Wyatt brushed the dust and grunge aside with his sleeve.

"Victor," Jim called. "Check this out."

The map was hand drawn with colored ink, graphically representing this entire sector. The academy was displayed in the map's center.

Jim laid a finger on the map.

"That would be where we came ashore," he said. The storm drain wasn't represented, but the beach was there. His finger drifted across the map. "And that is where we started inland."

Wyatt indicated the location of the governor's estate. On the map, it looked like a long way from the ancient academy.

Victor studied the landscape between academy and estate in silence; a dark wood, a band of foothills, a village. He recognized the name of the village: Malonar; it existed still.

Any villages may have been established since the creation of this ancient map wouldn't be shown here. Victor didn't know, as he was unfamiliar with this region.

Jim indicated the woods.

"Johnson Woods," he said. "I've heard of it."

"As have I," said Jim. It was named after a member of the original colonists. "They say there are bad things in there. No one goes in there."

"Bad things?" asked Victor. "That is rather ambiguous."

"I expect we'll find out, soon enough," Wyatt said, matter-of-factly.

"Yes. The woods are between us and home," agreed Jim.

Victor slowly looked away from the map. His attention was on the doors leading outside. He moved to the doors and stood to one side. He looked out through the grit and grime on the glass.

Jim watched curiously. He heard what Victor heard then; distant at first, it was coming nearer.

"A flyer..." he said softly.

"The Guild has expanded their search," said Wyatt.

Victor saw it. High overhead, the small, unmanned drone passed over the academy complex. It slowed and hovered a hundred yards distant, turned left and circled back. It followed a pattern for almost a minute before continuing on.

Victor waited until he was certain the flyer wasn't coming back, then looked back to Jim and Wyatt.

"This is likely part of a preliminary search pattern only," he said. "When they find no evidence of our travels, we should expect a more extensive search."

"They have a lot of ground to cover," said Jim. "They can't know exactly where we left the beach."

"They can guess." Wyatt moved to the doors and stood beside Victor. "And they know where we're going. Where else would we go?"

"Our options are indeed limited," agreed Victor. He indicated the map. "As are available routes."

Jim studied the map again, searching for possible alternatives. True enough. All alternatives were only minor deviations from the main route, no matter where they started from. Sooner or later, their pursuers would see that and would be waiting at key choke points along their path.

Their pursuers...

The Founders Guild had been operating under a truce with the Kimaran government for several years, its actions maybe ninety percent legal. That other ten percent was mostly activity in partnership with the Silver Pirates, a powerful arm of the Outworld Band. This relationship gave the Guild access to off-planet markets and gave the pirates access to the Kimaran market.

The Guild had no obvious reason to come after Jim. But they were.

It had to be the pirates. The slavers, with close ties to the pirates, had never been happy about having to give Jim up on ShadowWorld. And they weren't all that happy with Jim's attempts to take on the slaver network since then.

As the pirates had no way to get to Jim while he was on Kimara, they must have made the Guild an offer it couldn't refuse; an offer the Guild was willing to in all likelihood lose the truce over.

Not good for Jim.

He looked over at his friends.

Not good for them either.

He knew they would stand with him no matter what the threat, no matter what he said. Victor was his protector as well as a loyal friend. Wyatt was, well... Wyatt.

"Can we make it to the woods before dark?" he asked.

"We have several hours yet," said Victor.

"You want to spend the night in the woods?" asked Wyatt. "Really?"

"It would be harder to find us in there than in here, should they come looking for us."

"He's right," said Jim. "Let's go."

Chapter Five

After an hour's easy walk from the academy, they came to a large meadow of wildflowers of pink and purple and powder blue. It was near dusk. They crossed the meadow and approached a dark green forest wall eighty feet high. Entering the wood, the world was silent and still. Other than occasional clusters of giant Kimaran fern, the forest floor was bare and open, blanketed in a thick layer of mulch. Jim led the way, carrying the hand lantern. They walked in a hazy sphere of light, passing between thin gray tree trunks rising up to a dark canopy.

Another hour's walk and Jim came to a stop. He held the lantern out, left and then right; ahead again.

"What is it?" asked Wyatt.

"A trail," said Jim. A dirt trail that was clear of mulch approached from their left, continued ahead of them and disappeared in the gray shadowy forest.

"An animal trail," said Victor. He knelt down, indicated for Jim to hold the lantern low to the ground before them.

There were several different animal tracks in the hardened dirt of the well-traveled, well-worn trail.

Victor glanced up at Wyatt and gave him a questioning look.

"Sorry. I don't recognize them," said Wyatt. He looked about. "But I'm pretty sure I don't want to come face to face with whatever made 'em."

Jim looked up the trail. It was heading in their general direction.

"It looks to be going where we're going," he said. It made sense to Jim that an animal trail would go where animals wanted to go, so maybe it also went where Jim, Wyatt and Victor wanted to go.

Jim started walking. Wyatt and Victor followed close enough to stay in the light of the lantern that Jim was carrying. The trail soon led them to a creek running across their path. It was about thirty feet wide, ran clear. The animal trail turned left and followed the bank. There were paw prints all along the water's edge, but no sign of the animals that had made them.

Jim knelt at the bank and filled their water skins. With that done, they followed the trail along the creek looking for a way across. After a few hundred yards, Victor pointed to a rise off to their left, nearby but above and away from the creek. It was getting late, and they had been keeping an eye out for a place to spend the night.

They climbed up onto the rise and stepped out onto a level clearing. It was enclosed on two sides by clusters of fern, a third side by a couple of short trees. The fourth side opened out above the creek.

It looked like a good place to set up camp.

Despite being in the middle of a forest, they had a difficult time finding enough firewood and kindling to make a campfire. In the end they kept the fire small and ate another cold meal from their rations. They settled in for the night then, taking turns standing watch.

Jim and Wyatt lay asleep near the campfire, now down to glowing coals and an occasional flicker of orange and red flame. Victor stood several steps from the fire, his back to the camp, his eyes on the shadows in the surrounding trees.

From behind him came the soothing, pleasant, burbling sounds of the creek below the rise, as the water rolled gently over a bed of smooth river rock.

From the shadows in the forest before him came ominous, menacing animal sounds; guttural, throaty, deep growls.

For the moment those sounds came no nearer. Whatever creatures were stalking the night were keeping their distance. Perhaps their focus lay elsewhere, at least for now.

Jim rolled slowly onto his side and sat up. He looked first to Wyatt, who was lying under a light blanket on the other side of the campfire. He looked then to Victor, standing a few yards away, his back to the camp.

Jim leaned forward and stood then, took the several steps between them and stood beside Victor. Neither spoke at first; they were silent for long moments, listening to the sounds that were coming from the dark.

When Jim finally spoke, it was hardly above a whisper.

"That doesn't sound so good."

"Prey would agree with you."

"That tingling running up and down my spine suggests that we might fall into that category."

"Very few species are prey to none, Jim."

"That doesn't make me feel any better, Victor. You're not very good at this."

"My apologies," said Victor. He continued looking out at the shadows. "They do not approach. They are likely pursuing more familiar prey."

Jim thought on that.

"Okay, that helps," he said. "Just a little. Thanks."

"Of course, Jim."

At that moment there came a deeper, darker, more menacing growl. The world immediately went dead quiet. It was a heavy silence, leaving only the sounds of the burbling of creek behind them.

"Uh, oh," said Jim.

"Yes."

A long pause, then...

"That is sooo quiet," whispered Jim.

"Yes."

"I liked the animal sounds better."

"Yes," said Victor. "The silence is rather unsettling."

"You said it."

"Yes. I did," Victor stated flatly.

Behind them, Wyatt was still sleeping.

Jim had always envied Wyatt's ability to sleep no matter the circumstance. He was comfortable with the knowledge that his friends would watch over him and wake him if necessary.

Jim certainly had faith in Victor and Wyatt, but...

"I think I'm done with sleep for tonight," said Jim.

The rest of the night passed without incident. They started out again early the next morning once the darkest of the night had turned a dark gray. They hadn't gone more than a few hundred yards when they came upon a large deciduous tree, standing alone, growing where the bank sloped steeply to the water's edge, the thick branches of the tree's canopy reaching out over the creek. A cliff rose up from the water on the opposite bank, a narrow ledge half a dozen feet below the top of the thirty foot bluff.

Jim moved into the clearing and then beneath the tree. He felt the cool moisture rising up from the creek beside him. He turned about and watched Wyatt step up to the bank and study the creek further downstream; he watched as Victor walked the perimeter of the clearing and looked into the woods and clusters of giant fern.

Both then returned to stand with Jim beneath the tree.

Wyatt noted that the creek didn't look to be any easier to cross further on. Victor noted the animal trail they had been following fizzled out not far beyond the clearing, while a number of lesser trails ran into the clearing from a number of directions.

For Jim, this all suggested that this clearing was intended as the final destination of whatever lived in these woods.

Wyatt likely thought the same.

"So where does this leave us?" he asked.

Jim placed a hand on the large trunk of the towering tree, looked out across the creek. It was only about twenty feet wide at this point, but there was no bank on the other side. The cliff rose directly out of the water, with a narrow ledge several dozen feet up the bluff, about six feet below the top.

He looked back then the way they had come.

"Maybe we should backtrack," he suggested. There had been several places where they could have crossed.

"That may no longer be an option," Victor stated coolly. He was looking up the trail.

Jim saw nothing. "What is it?" he asked.

"Something approaches," said Victor. He unsheathed his pair of staff weapons.

Seeing that, Wyatt lifted his hand sling from his belt, brought out two stones and loaded one of them into the sling pouch. He stepped away from Jim and Victor.

"Whatcha' hearing, Victor?"

"There are several of them," said Victor. "Beyond that, I cannot say."

Jim stepped away from the tree. He moved to one side of Wyatt. The sounds were very similar to what they had heard during the night.

Victor cocked his head smoothly then, let his gaze drift along the perimeter of the clearing, into the surrounding forest.

"Victor?" asked Jim.

"Yes," stated Victor.

"Oh, boy..."

"Yes." Victor let his senses stretch away from the clearing. "Another eight or ten."

"Okay," sighed Wyatt. "Let's do this."

Jim saw moving shadows in the woods; dog size, a bit larger. Their slow movements were as yet stealthy.

"Only ten, huh?" said Jim.

"And those coming up the trail," Victor responded matter-of-factly.

The shadows continued to close in on the clearing.

"So only twelve then," said Wyatt, attempting humor.

"Perhaps more." Victor didn't get the humor.

Wyatt brought out another two stones; three now in his hand, one in the sling pocket.

Jim quietly considered.

"We're going to lose this," he stated. He looked about them. "We need an alternative."

"Not many of those," said Wyatt. "We're pretty much surrounded."

Jim looked behind them, to the creek; across the creek. "Not completely."

Wyatt glanced quickly behind them, back again to the impending threat. "That's a creek and a cliff."

"An alternative," said Jim.

"It is an option," agreed Victor.

The first of the creatures stepped into the clearing. It looked a little like a rat, especially the head, but it was the size of a large wolf. Its short, coarse hair was brown and gray, fell and rose along the animal's spine as it moved writhe-like into the open space.

Wyatt glanced again behind them, to the creek, to the cliff wall opposite. He looked again at the creature.

Another creature stepped in beside the first. It was just as large, just as menacing.

"All right," he said, more determined. "I am recalculating the odds of surviving our two options."

"And what does your math tell you?"

A creature appeared at the trailhead of the path they had been following along the creek. It stepped fully into the clearing.

It had been following them.

"I vote for getting wet," said Wyatt.

"Yes," Victor stated firmly.

Two more of the creatures stepped into the clearing. They began moving apart as they moved forward; a unified pattern.

Jim stepped backward in the direction of the water.

"Into the creek then," he said.

"Yes," Victor said again. He sheathed his short staff weapons.

Wyatt put his ammo stones back into his pocket, hooked his sling back onto his belt. Stepping back, he picked up the canvas bag, hooked a loop over his shoulder.

"Ready when you are," he said, took another step back. His heels touched the water.

Jim and Victor moved slowly back until they were standing to either side of Wyatt. More of the creatures came into the clearing. Three of the nearer animals lifted a single front paw and sat stock-still.

"Let's go," Jim hissed, turned and ran into the creek. His friends followed after him.

They pushed ahead in the water, feet pushing against the creek-bed. Behind them, the sounds of the onrushing pack of creatures, their claws tearing at the grassy ground of the clearing, their growls growing to the call of the attack.

The water level reached Jim's chest and he began using his arms to help move him forward, scooping at the water with his hands and pulling as he pushed off with his feet and legs. Victor passed him on his left, Wyatt struggled beside him on his right.

Jim heard splashing behind them. As best he could tell, only two or three of the creatures had followed them into the creek. He reached out then and grabbed at the cliff. Finding handholds, he pulled himself close to the rock wall.

He took a moment then to look back over his shoulder. Three of the creatures were two-thirds of the way across the creek, would be on them in seconds. The others, seven or eight at least, were hopping up and down on the bank, howling and yelping.

"Climb!" Victor called out. He was already fully out of the water.

Jim climbed quickly. On his right, Wyatt was pulling himself out of the water, the wet canvas bag looking to be pulling him down.

Fully out of the water now, Jim looked below him. One of the creatures was scraping at the cliff just below his feet.

Wyatt began crying out angrily, kicking at a creature that was pawing at him before pulling himself up and out of reach.

Jim continued then up the cliff. Moments later, he felt Victor grasp him under his arm and pull him up onto the ledge.

"Some help, here," Wyatt called. Victor stepped around Jim and pulled Wyatt up.

Jim, sitting with his feet hanging over the ledge, looked down at the three creatures clawing at the cliff below them. One had managed to creep part way out of the water. It lost its grasp and splashed back into the creek.

Once the creatures realized there was no hope, they worked their way back to their comrades on the bank. All then sat in line, grew quiet; they silently eyed those on the ledge.

"What are they waiting for?" asked Jim.

"Lunch," said Wyatt.

Jim looked up and behind them. It was only another six feet to the top of the cliff.

"Let's remove ourselves from the menu," he said.

Victor stood and reached up over the lip of the cliff. He had to find a foothold before he was able to pull himself up and over. He turned and went to his knees, held a hand out to Jim.

"Up you come, Jim."

Once all three were off the cliff, they stood side by side and looked at where they had yet to go; through a forest of widely scattered trees, thickly clustered fern and broad-leaved shrubs. Beyond the woods, no more than a thousand yards or so away, they could see the tops of rolling foothills.

They would be out of Johnson Wood by midday. After the morning they had already been through, they would stop for the day once they were out. They would get an early start across the foothills the next morning.

Chapter Six

"Let's take a break," said Jim.

Victor indicated a grove of scraggy, twisted trees not far up ahead.

"Just a bit further," he suggested.

Jim nodded in answer and they kept walking. They had been working their way through grassy foothills for hours. There had been very little cover since leaving Johnson Wood, should a Guild flyer pass overhead.

They entered the small grove and dropped their gear. The trees were clustered together in a shallow basin between two of the gently rolling hills. There were several dozen trees of misshapen gray-brown trunks and thick branches, with canopies of broad, yellow-green leaves.

They settled in at the base of one of the trees for their first break of the day. There had been no sign that they were being pursued, and they hadn't seen a flyer since the academy.

Jim uncapped one of the water skins and took a swallow. He handed the water skin to Wyatt.

"How much further, do you think?" he asked.

"To the village?" Wyatt took a swallow of water and passed the skin to Victor. "We won't make it today. Tomorrow morning, I figure."

Jim nodded. "So we hike it as far as we can till dark, find a little hidey-hole to spend the night, start out again at dawn."

"Agreed," said Wyatt.

"Yes." Victor capped the water skin, set it beside the knapsacks. He slid back and rested against a tree trunk. He closed his eyes.

This would be a short break, so Jim and Wyatt were careful not to get too comfortable. If they rested for more than a few minutes, they were afraid their bodies would take it as a sign and shut down for the day.

So after another five minutes, Jim shifted to his knees and stood up, signaling that it was time to move on. He handed one of the knapsacks to Victor, grabbed the other pack and the water skin. They continued to follow the floor of the narrow gorge. The walls grew steeper and higher, the ravine narrower and darker. They walked in the cool of the shade, the sun's rays unable reach the floor.

An hour further into the ravine, Victor reached out and placed a hand on Jim's arm. They stopped and Jim looked back to Victor, questioning. Victor nodded ahead.

Jim turned forward again and all three went to their knees, looked warily ahead.

There was a loud hum, almost a buzz, but Jim couldn't see where it was coming from. He gave another questioning look to Victor.

"Twenty paces ahead," said Victor. "I do not know what it is."

"It's a ground bee nest," stated Wyatt.

"Ground bees? You sure?" Jim knew of ground bees of course, but had never seen one, and had certainly never run across one of their nests. His life on Kimara over the previous two years had been limited to the Governor's estate, the Academy, and the journeys across the inland sea every three months.

"Ground bees," said Wyatt. "There's no other sound quite like it."

Victor scooted around Jim and slid cautiously forward, studied the route ahead. He slid another few feet and stopped.

There...

Fifty feet ahead, in a shallow hollow along the left wall, about four feet above the floor of the ravine... dark shadows were bustling in a dark, thick mass; but the nest was still too far away for him to see anything clearly.

Victor looked above them, studied possible routes up and along the walls of the gorge.

He scooted back then and rejoined the others.

"Well?" asked Jim.

"We go up and around," said Victor. "There is an easy path up the right wall to the top of the ridge. We avoid the ground bee nest."

The decision made, Victor led the way across the narrow floor and to the path running up the wall. As they climbed, the humming, buzzing sound of the nest below them faded. Reaching the top of the wall, they began following the ridge.

They stopped when they were directly opposite the nest. Jim dropped to his knees, then onto his belly, and looked down to the floor of the ravine. He scrutinized the opposite wall near the floor.

There it is...

A hole in the wall, eighteen inches across, several feet above the floor, black, in heavy shadow. Moving all about the hole, in and out of the hole, were dozens of fuzzy black balls with yellow stripes across their backs. They were four to six inches in diameter, with two pairs of large transparent wings.

"Yep," Wyatt sighed. "Them's ground bees."

"I didn't realize they were so big," said Jim.

"With stingers to match," said Wyatt. "They can sting, they can bite; their choice. Either one can take you down. More than one of either can kill you."

"So I understand," said Victor.

"All right." Jim scooted back and stood up. "Let's get out of here."

Following the ridge, the ravine grew increasingly shallow and they slowly descended toward the ravine floor. A hundred yards further on, the gorge wall fell away to a gentle slope. They came to a cluster of short, twisted trees growing along the hillside.

Another sound then, barely discernable even to Victor's keen ears. He turned about and went to one knee, just in the shadow of the trees. The others knelt down beside him.

A small drone flyer was following the ravine, traveling slow, coming in their direction. Jim, Wyatt and Victor remained motionless, knowing that any movement would be caught by the flyer's sensors.

As slow as it was traveling, it slowed further still as it neared. It stopped then, hovered, thirty feet from the grove, a hundred feet in the air.

"Uh, oh," mumbled Jim. The flyer's sensors had picked them up.

"Well said, my friend," mumbled Wyatt.

The flyer suddenly and quickly rose up another hundred feet into the sky and then turned away.

"We can expect company," said Victor.

Wyatt stood and walked out of the grove. He glanced up into the clear blue sky, then back up the ravine. Jim and Victor moved up to stand beside him.

Victor was studying their path ahead.

"What are you thinking?" Jim asked him.

"The flyer will be under the direction of a team. They are likely on foot."

"Following our most likely path," said Jim.

"Yes."

Wyatt took another step forward. His focused shifted from the ravine floor to the ridge along the wall, back then to the floor behind them, to what now lay just beyond their sight.

"I think they should get acquainted with our new friends," he said, almost to himself.

"Are you thinking..." wondered Jim.

"I'm always thinking."

Victor studied the terrain before them. Suspecting what Wyatt had in mind, he was already planning their return along the ridgeline and to their viewpoint above the ground bee nest.

§

Jim, Wyatt and Victor were on their elbows and bellies looking over the ridge and down into the ravine, once again directly opposite the ground bee nest.

After half an hour of patiently waiting, Jim began to wonder whether they had misread the whole thing. Maybe the flyer hadn't seen them, or maybe the Guild was so far away that it would have been better for them to have made a run for it.

Then of course, if they did show up, was this really a good idea?

"Wyatt... are you sure about this?" asked Jim.

"Oh, I am soooo sure," said Wyatt.

"Right," said Jim. "You fill me with confidence."

"I'm glad to help, Jim."

"I suggest quiet," said Victor, his tone hushed and at the same time forceful.

Wyatt put on a sheepish grin, while Jim looked curiously over at Victor, then down into the ravine. He didn't see anything, didn't hear anything.

But of course Victor had surprising hearing and vision...

So they waited.

Several more minutes passed.

Victor gave a nod then, indicating the ravine floor near the bend far up from the location of the nest. At first Jim saw nothing, but after a few more moments he saw several figures in the shadows. Moments more and there were several more figures.

A group of men and women were working their way up the ravine.

Beside Jim, Wyatt brought up his hand sling and a stone. He held it ready.

The Guild team stopped.

No, no, no... Jim's jaws tightened. *Keep walking...*

They were about forty feet from the nest. They could certainly hear the ground bees.

They need to be closer; they must get closer.

One of the Guild team started forward, hesitantly, followed moments later by the others.

Three steps, four steps...

The lead team member slowed.

Five steps, six.

They were now about twenty five feet from the ground bee nest.

They took another step. They stopped.

"Now, Wyatt," said Victor.

Wyatt stood up and readied his sling, dropped the stone in the pocket. He held the sling out, weighed the stone. He moved his weapon hand side to side, gave two quick spins and let it loose.

The stone struck the nest, struck one of the ground bees.

The nest went crazy. The cloud of ground bees grew, rushing from the nest, seeking out the threat to their home, the source of the assault, and found it twenty two feet away on the ravine floor.

The approaching group of guild members.

Jim and Victor slid back from the ridge and stood as Wyatt stepped back. They hurried away, the way they had come, the sounds of screams and angry cries following them.

They did not want to see the results of what they had done. Success or no, there was no upside to waiting around.

Chapter Seven

Wyatt walked across the clearing to where Jim lay asleep under a thin blanket. He went to one knee and placed a hand on Jim's shoulder. Jim growled lightly and opened his eyes; Wyatt walked over to the pair of knapsacks, opened one and began rummaging inside.

Jim sat up and looked about the clearing. It was early morning. The air was cool, the sky slate gray, clear. The sun had yet to show itself.

There was no sign of Victor; *probably making his rounds.*

They had stopped for the night just after dusk when they came to this cluster of trees and heavy brush nestled in a hollow, with hills rising on all sides. It would provide them with safe cover.

Each had stood watch for several hours. It had been a quiet night.

Jim looked into the shadows of the surrounding trees and brush.

"Where's Victor?" he asked.

"He's checking our route ahead."

Wyatt returned to Jim with a package of dried fruit and a wedge of cheese. He sat beside him and they quietly ate breakfast.

They were getting low on food, but they expected to reach the village by midmorning so didn't worry about rationing. They could resupply there before continuing, or send word to the governor and wait to get picked up.

Victor came into the clearing. He settled in beside the others without a word and accepted a piece of cheese from Wyatt.

Once they were finished with breakfast, they gathered what little remained of their gear and supplies and started out, following the path that Victor had trail-blazed out of the hollow. They were soon forced to climb the slope up a hillside, then traveled along just below the ridgeline as far as it took them. The rolling hills here were covered in tall grass with very little brush and very few trees.

The sun rose and the day turned bright, the hills shimmering yellow. The cool air warmed and the moisture in the air slowly evaporated. An hour later they found themselves walking the floor of a narrow gorge. It wound between one set of hills after another. They passed an occasional tree, an occasional cluster of brush. They stopped once for a brief water break before continuing on.

They came out of the mouth of the gorge midmorning. Ahead was a valley, the floor a thousand yards wide at its widest. A green mountain range rose high on the left. Rolling hills one after another bordered the valley on the right, these covered in deciduous trees and thick brush.

Jim looked down into the heart of the valley. Dozens of rooftops, dozens of designs, were arrayed in no apparent pattern. The village was too far away for him to see much detail beyond the occasional pedestrian street. Columns of smoke rose from a handful of chimneys.

"Waddya see, Victor?" he asked.

Victor studied the scene, looking for any sign of bad guys.

"All is quiet," he said. "I think we're good."

Jim accepted that and started down the narrow, winding path toward the village. Approaching the first buildings, two children came out of the nearest and watched the visitors from the porch. They were dressed in the familiar Kimaran garb of leather, cotton and wool. They stood silent as the strangers passed. Wyatt gave them a wink.

The children did not respond, despite Wyatt clearly being a Kimaran, seemingly *one of them*.

Kimaran maybe, but one of them? This village was isolated; strangers were likely rare.

They turned down a wide pedestrian street and followed it toward the middle of the village. Well-maintained wooden storefronts lined the way. Townsfolk silently watched the strangers from shadowed porches. Their clothes were simple, clean and of quality.

Jim led the way into the central plaza. The curious, wary villagers kept their distance.

A tall, thin man in loose leather pants and shirt came out of the town hall, the building being a simple structure with narrow windows set to either side of a heavy door. He stepped down from the porch, wooden staff in hand, walked across the plaza and stood before the newcomers. He was clean-shaven, his brown hair pulled back tight and tied in a long ponytail.

He indicated the circle of villagers hovering about at a distance.

"Excuse them," he said. "We don't get many visitors."

"I understand," said Jim. "I'm Jim."

"Yes. Son of the governor."

"That's right," Jim said cautiously.

"I'm Jonas, mayor of Malonar. Welcome." Jonas shook Jim's hand, then shook hands with Wyatt and Victor, who introduced themselves. The mayor gave a familiar nod to Wyatt, one Kimaran to another.

He didn't seem at all surprised with Victor's alien appearance.

"How can we be of service?" he asked, looking again to Jim.

"We need to contact the governor," said Jim.

"We will do our best," said Jonas. "I must warn you, however, that communication with the capital is less than reliable."

"I understand." Such was common on Kimara when not using landlines.

"You are welcome to stay as long as you like."

"I don't think that's a good idea," said Wyatt. He was concerned that their presence would bring nothing but bad down on the village.

Victor believed this as well. Whether they managed to reach the governor or not, they should continue on, draw those following them away from the village.

He suggested as much, and Jim agreed.

"As you believe best," said the mayor. He offered to take Wyatt to the seldom-used communication station; he then waved one of the nearby villagers over. Jim and Victor would be escorted to the village's one and only guest house, where they might clean up and have something to eat.

Jim watched the mayor lead Wyatt back toward the town hall building, then he and Victor followed their escort in the other direction through the circle of villagers and down a side street. They approached a small, square, nondescript building.

"Here you are." The escort opened the door and stepped aside. Jim and Victor entered.

The guest house had a main room, a small sleeping room, and a bathroom closet. The main room was furnished with a table and chairs on the right, a couch and two chairs on the left. There was a wash basin, soap and towels on a counter.

Jim tossed his knapsack onto one of the chairs, looked back to the escort standing in the open doorway.

"Thank you," he said.

The escort gave a nod in answer, turned away and stepped off the porch. Victor closed the door, looked back into the room. Natural light streamed in through the windows.

"If we are here when the Guild arrives, the villagers will be put at risk," he said.

What would the Guild do if they thought Jim was in the village, even perhaps being hidden by the villagers?

Jim stood at the wash basin, turned on the water and began cleaning up.

"We'll leave as soon as we collect supplies," he said.

§

Wyatt came into the guest house carrying a basket of assorted meats, fruits and breads. "Lunch is served." He set the basket on the table.

"Were you able to—" Jim started, his words cut off mid-sentence.

"Nothing but static." Wyatt went to the counter and began washing his hands and face. "Jonas promised to keep trying."

That last comment made it clear to Jim that Wyatt agreed they should move on as quickly as possible. If and when the mayor finally managed to make contact with the governor, he would let him know where to look for them.

"That works for me." Jim began sorting through the basket.

Looking to the open doors of the sleeping room and the bathroom closet, Wyatt realized that Victor wasn't there.

"Victor?"

Jim nodded to the front door as he prepared a plate for himself.

"He's out getting supplies." Even as Jim said this, Victor came through the door with both knapsacks filled. He set them on the floor against the wall and joined the others at the table. They sat and finished serving themselves.

Victor lifted a brow to Wyatt, who shook his head no. Victor was not in the least surprised.

They made their plans as they ate. They would leave the village immediately after finishing lunch. Wyatt would meet with the mayor on the way out and let him know they were moving on. Should the Guild team show up, which they had no doubt they would, the mayor was to be open with them.

Yes, Jim and his friends had been there; they had collected supplies and had continued on.

And so there would be no reason for the Guild to take action against the village.

"These are good people," said Wyatt. He had quickly become friends with several of the villagers, despite their wariness of strangers. The thought that they might be responsible for bringing danger to the townspeople disturbed him.

Victor sensed Wyatt's concern.

"The Guild's search would bring them to the village no matter our decision to come here," he said. "The village is along our path."

The logic did not make Wyatt feel any better. They were the target of and the reason for the Guild's search, and so were still responsible for the Guild coming to the village.

"I'm sure they'll be okay," said Jim. While the Founders Guild often operated in the shadows, they were seldom violent, whatever their most recent actions might suggest. Guild interests necessitated an accord with the Kimaran government that would be put at risk if the Guild became overtly aggressive.

They finished their lunch, then cleared away the table and packed their gear and supplies. Ready then, they stepped out onto the porch. Jim closed the door and moved to the top step.

"We ready?" he asked.

"Let's do this," said Wyatt. He stepped down from porch. "I'll meet you at the trailhead."

Jim and Victor watched Wyatt start up the street to the town hall, then they too stepped down from the porch and started in the other direction toward the edge of town.

Chapter Eight

A group of eight men and women came out of the mouth of the gorge and stopped at the head of the wide, winding path that led down to the small, isolated village of Malonar. The Guild team leader studied the cluster of buildings that was spread across the floor of the valley, the rest of his team standing behind him, glad of the opportunity to take a break.

They were one of two ground teams that were pursuing the governor's son, and they had grown more vigilant after hearing of the unexpected attack on the first team, which had slowed their pace. To have any hope of catching up with their quarry, they had taken very few breaks over the previous several days, had traveled late into each night, and had started out each day well before dawn.

A search probe passed overhead and continued on toward the village below. The sensors of the Guild flyer were being monitored by one of the team members, a young woman wearing a headset with an eyepiece, earpiece and small microphone. The full sensor gear was contained in the small backpack she was wearing.

The team leader started forward again, leading the others down the path to the village, following after the flyer.

The streets were quiet. What villagers they saw were watching from behind closed windows, from doorways with doors standing slightly ajar. The team traveled cautiously, wary for any signs of danger. There was no real reason to expect an attack from these simple villagers, but who knew what the governor's son might have stirred up; and of course just look at what had happened to the other team.

They entered the main plaza. It was empty but for one man standing in the heart of the square. He had clearly been waiting for their arrival. The mayor held his hands clasped in front of him, and gave a slight nod of welcome as they approached.

There was a silent exchange between guild leader and village mayor.

Jim and Wyatt followed Victor across the open field to the square stone and mortar structure that stood alone in the short yellow grass. The station was three days out from the village, and was exactly where the mayor had told them they would find it.

Victor pointed to the left as he approached the building, directing the others to the hand pump of the water well as he continued to the heavy wooden door.

Wyatt handed one of the water skins to Jim.

"Here ya go," he said, and followed Victor.

"Right," said Jim wearily, and went to the pump. After three days on the trail, both skins needed filling.

He had only just begun working the pump handle when his friends came out of the building and joined him.

"So?" he asked.

"No," said Wyatt.

Jim wanted more than a simple no. He looked to Victor.

"The communications equipment is no longer in operating condition," said Victor.

"As we expected," said Wyatt.

True, thought Jim. *But I hoped...*

He returned to pumping the handle. A strong stream of water spewed from the faucet. Wyatt picked up one of the water skins, watched and waited until the water ran clean. He then held the bag under the faucet.

The emergency station was old, very old. It was situated mid-distance between four or five key locations from the distant past. It had a communications station, emergency supplies, food and clothing.

Or it had at one time, but hadn't been maintained for years. The well was there, with a working hand pump. Inside the building were two shelves of clothing in sealed packaging. Whatever preserved rations there might once have been was long gone, as were the first aid supplies.

And, as Victor had said, the communications equipment was no longer functioning. It was all there, but it wasn't working.

They finished filling the water skins. Jim took a step from the pump as Wyatt stood and set the skins aside.

"All right," said Wyatt. "So, what do we do?"

"We go on," said Jim. "We've another two or three hours till dark."

"We could wait here," suggested Wyatt. "Your father will know we came this way."

"You are assuming that Mayor Jonas has successfully communicated with the capital," said Victor.

"I'm assuming nothing," said Wyatt. "If the Governor's Guard believes we are attempting to get home, as they would, then they will look here. This station is a logical location to check."

"Perhaps," Victor said calmly. "That being so, the same must be said of the Guild."

And we know the Guild is not far behind us, thought Jim.

"We go on," Jim said again.

"Very well; this way, then," said Victor.

They gathered up their gear and started across the clearing toward the trailhead. Victor led the way in, carefully eyeing the brush on either side as they continued along the trail, what little trail there was. Likely only used by animals for who knew how many years, there really wasn't much of a trail to follow.

Victor stopped. He slowly raised a hand. Jim, directly behind him, and Wyatt, bringing up the rear, both stopped. Both looked ahead past Victor, then into the vegetation to either side.

They saw nothing, heard nothing.

Victor, however, had seen something...

The thick shrub just ahead and on the left: there was a freshly broken branch, chest high.

Jim watched Victor calmly reach back to bring out his pair of weapon staffs, then hesitate, then slowly lower his hands without his weapons.

"Victor..." Jim said softly. Behind him, he heard Wyatt take a short step back.

"Stand down, Jim," said Victor. He held his hands out in a sign of capitulation.

Jim went numb... for Victor to submit meant there was no alternative.

A voice came from the brush. "Good call, my friend." The words were spoken in a calm, confident tone.

There was a sudden onrush of motion and sound. Jim watched two people grasp at Victor, heard a struggle behind him as Wyatt was taken. Jim held his arms out and to the side.

A man stepped around Victor and stood in front of Jim. He wore a slight smile.

"Good afternoon, young man." The Guild team leader clasped his hands behind him, gave a slight nod. "You have been a bit of trouble, have you not? I'm sure you appreciate."

"Great. Glad to hear it," said Jim. He kept an eye beyond the man, to Victor. He would take his cue from his friend. Victor's temporary acceptance of the situation was simply that: temporary. He would be ever watchful for an opportunity to safely free Jim before the Founders Guild could turn him over to the pirates.

"No doubt," said the man. "In any case, look about you. Witness the outcome."

The outcome is yet to be decided, thought Jim. He gave a thin smile.

"Right," he said softly.

The man kept his focus on Jim as his team disarmed the captives.

He took a step aside then and indicated the trail ahead.

"Shall we?" he offered.

"Right," Jim said again.

§

The village mayor and the commander of the Governor's Guard walked across the lobby together and stepped out onto the porch of the village's town hall. The meeting had been brief, the mayor providing what little information he had regarding Jim and his friends, and of the Guild team's visit several days before.

"Do not apologize, Jonas," said Commander Thornton. "You did right; exactly as you were asked to do."

"I can't help but be concerned for their wellbeing," said the Mayor. "Such fine young people."

"That they are." William Thornton was a big man with an imposing presence. He had been the commander of the Governor's Guard for six years, since well before the current governor's arrival on Kimara. The Guard was his life, all the better that he liked and respected the current governor. He also liked the boy. Jim was a good kid.

The boy and his friends had left the village four days earlier. The Guild team had come and gone only a day behind them. The mayor had managed to communicate with the governor's estate a day later, albeit only briefly, just long enough to let the Guard know that Jim had come and gone.

Commander Thornton let his gaze drift upward, beyond the village plaza, beyond the village rooftops.

There was a chance that young Jim was still free, may have eluded his pursuers. Just as likely, however, the Guild had captured him and his comrades. They hadn't been far behind, and knew just where they were going.

Captured or no, Jim would be rescued, would be returned to his family. Of that, Commander Thornton had no doubt.

He looked again about the plaza. A number of villagers were gathered in small groups, curious at yet more visitors to their isolated community.

They almost never had visitors; now three times in less than a week; this latest group arriving by transport flyer, which had landed just outside the village.

There were wary glances up at the man who was standing beside the mayor on the porch.

Thornton noted then three of his team coming into the plaza from a side street. Understanding the village's isolation, they had brought supplies they knew the village could use, supplies they couldn't produce themselves. Thornton's people had been busy transferring these supplies to appropriate supply houses and distribution facilities throughout the village.

His team started up the main thoroughfare toward their flyer.

"We thank you for the supplies," said the mayor. "We have been lacking in a number of things."

"Of course, Jonas," said Thornton. Being originally from a small, isolated town himself, William Thornton understood the difficulties such villages often faced. "We would have been remiss to have arrived emptyhanded."

"You're a good friend, Will," said the mayor.

Thornton briefly placed a hand on the mayor's shoulder. "I have been much too negligent a friend, Jonas. When did I last visit?"

Jonas thought a moment, smiled then, "Carla's birthday?"

"Ah. Yes," Thornton said in a heavy sigh. Carla was the mayor's daughter, Thornton's goddaughter. She had come of age this past year. She was engaged to be married the next spring. "She is well?"

"She is. Word has been sent." Jonas looked out across the plaza, seeking his daughter.

"I do hope to see her before I leave," said Thornton.

"She would be sorry to miss you, but time is critical."

"That it is." Thornton understood that successfully recovering Jim and his comrades could come down to a matter of minutes.

Another of Thornton's team crossed the plaza and came to the foot of the steps. He placed one foot on the bottom step and gave a sharp nod to Thornton.

"Comm is installed, up and running, Commander."

"Good work, Franklin," said Thornton.

"Yes," said Mayor Jonas. "Very much appreciated."

In addition to the other supplies, the Guard had brought new communications equipment. Franklin had spent the last hour installing it.

"My pleasure, Mayor," said Franklin. They all understood that the new equipment would not guarantee communications with the outside world, but the quality and reliability of any connection would be much improved.

"Were you able to contact base?" Thornton asked.

"Briefly, commander," said Franklin. "No news. You are to take whatever actions you deem appropriate."

"Thank you, Franklin." Thornton frowned and dismissed Franklin with a nod, watched him back away from the steps and start across the plaza.

No news, Franklin had said. If there had been word regarding Captain Bellamy and his crew, that would have been news. That meant there had been no word; that meant Bellamy could be anywhere, or nowhere.

David R. Beshears

Chapter Nine

Jim rolled onto his side, pushed himself up onto one elbow, shifted about then and sat up. Victor was sitting beside him, ever watchful; Wyatt was asleep on the other side of Victor.

Jim pulled at a chain that was connected to a metal anklet on his left ankle. The chain bound Jim to Victor, and bound Victor to Wyatt.

Victor gave Jim a slight nod in a silent *good morning.* He had probably been awake most of the night.

Jim gave a nod in reply, looked then about the clearing. It was early morning, not yet dawn. One of the Guild team was sitting nearby at watch. The man eyed Jim sleepily, his forearms resting on his knees.

Several other of the Guild team were moving about the campsite; most were asleep under light blankets. The perimeter of the clearing was thick with brush. Overhead, the night sky was slowly giving way to predawn gray.

One of the abductors was kneeling beside the campfire pit. He worked at the dying coals and brought them back to life. He then prepared three metal coffee pots and set them onto heat stones that were evenly spaced within the circular fire pit.

This brought several of the team out from under their blankets. Most sat and sleepily watched, blankets wrapped about their shoulders; one stood and began moving slowly about the camp, kicking lightly at the bodies of those still sleeping.

Jim grumbled under his breath. "So begins another bright and cheery day on Kimara."

Victor looked side-glance to Jim, looked curiously to those moving about the campsite, outward then into the shadows beyond the clearing.

The day to come was likely to be neither bright nor cheery.

He looked again to Jim. He understood that the comment had been sarcasm and so considered responding with a sharp retort. Had Wyatt been awake, he would have responded with something clever.

Unfortunately, Victor could think of nothing witty to say.

"Yes. Quite," he said feebly.

It was another minute before the smell of brewing coffee drew Wyatt out from under his blanket. He sat up, scratched at his scalp, rubbed his face with both hands and looked about the camp.

"What's for breakfast?" he asked sleepily.

"As yet, I'm not seeing anything but coffee," said Victor.

"If we'll be offered even that," said Jim.

Their guard watched his charges without emotion, listened to their exchange without really listening. It just wasn't important. *They* weren't important beyond their value to their client, the pirates.

Jim saw that, sensed that. He had felt that same dismissive sentiment from all their captors the day before as they had been marched west toward what had been referred to as the *'pickup site'*, where they were to be handed off to whoever would then be turning them over to the pirates.

Jim made a show of not caring what the guard thought; he looked away from him and back into the camp. Several of the Guild team were quietly closing in on the coffee pots. Jim saw then another guildsman moving about the camp, taking large biscuits out of a bag and handing one to each of his comrades. Passing the three prisoners, he absently tossed three in their general direction, one after the other, one biscuit each.

Jim managed to catch his out of the air. He held it up to his nose, smelled it. He took a bite.

Wheat, rich butter, malted sugar, salt; heavy, thick consistency. It would definitely be filling.

He chewed, swallowed, took another bite.

"Not bad," he said quietly, chewing. Victor was already two bites into his own. Wyatt sniffed his biscuit warily, finally took a cautious bite.

He frowned, shrugged a shoulder. "Eh..."

Jim kept eating. He watched the leader of their captors move through his team and kneel at the fire pit. He poured himself a cup of coffee and stood. He took a sip, looked over the rim of the cup to Jim.

He said something then to the man standing beside him and indicated the prisoners. The man filled three cups and brought them over to Jim and his friends. His expression revealed nothing. He turned away without comment, returned to the campfire to get a cup of coffee for himself.

The leader rested his free hand on the man's shoulder as he addressed the entire clearing.

"Okay... pick it up, people," he said without raising his voice. "We move out in twenty."

Captain Bellamy knelt behind a short wall of brush, mostly Kimaran Fern, and settled in beside his first mate. The rest of the ship's crew were kneeling behind the nearby brush and trees to his left and right; silent, unmoving, watchful.

Forty yards beyond, the Guild team was following a winding trail through the forest of thin trees, fern and slough. Jim and his two companions walked with them, chained together at the ankles. The line of men and women moved in and out of sunlight and shadows at a steady pace.

Captain Bellamy studied the group for a few moments, looked then to his own crew.

It had been a circuitous journey that had brought them here.

The initial confrontation aboard the Governor's yacht had been brief, and his crew had been able to push the attackers back onto their own ship, then followed after them. During the melee, Bellamy's first mate had cut the boarding lines and pushed the ships apart. He then quickly damaged the wheel and rudder, effectively setting them adrift.

The fighting had continued for some time and the ship eventually ran aground a hundred feet from the beach. Despite a number of injuries, both sides had jumped ship and worked their way ashore. The guildsmen had immediately gone inland, disappearing into the woods. Bellamy and his crew had stayed on the beach, taking time to care for the wounded and regroup.

They started out a day later, following on the trail of the guildsmen. They were easy enough to track, but being a day ahead it was unlikely they would catch up to them for some time.

After a few days travel they observed several craft pass overhead. They were Governor's Guard, and looked to be heading in the direction of the village of Malonar.

They came across the fresh trail of another group a day later, the tracks no more than a few hours old. Captain Bellamy was certain they were Guild, and that they were following after Jim. If that were so, they were a much greater threat than the guildsmen from the ship.

He had been right. They caught up with this group two days after they had captured Jim and his friends.

For the moment, they would follow quietly and stay out of sight, watch for an opportunity to rescue Jim.

The Guild team stopped midday, the leader directing a guard to be posted ahead, another behind them back along the trail, and a guard to either side. Jim, Victor and Wyatt settled down at a wide spot in the trail, finding a slight rise to sit on.

They took swallows from their water skins and waited for the food rations to be handed out. Wyatt pushed the chain aside with his foot, frowned as he looked up and down the trail. There had been zero opportunity to escape to now, and he didn't see that there would be much chance in the future.

Whatever lay ahead for them, he didn't see any way of avoiding it.

Wyatt watched then as one of their abductors played with the sling that he had taken from him when they were first captured. The man struggled awkwardly with it, twirled it about with a stone in the pocket. He had no idea what he was doing and nearly struck the young woman standing next to him. The woman glared at him and moved further away.

Jim, looking up the trail, gave Wyatt a nudge with his elbow.

"What do you make of that?" he asked.

Wyatt looked where Jim indicated. The man who had been walking point well ahead of the group had returned and was talking with Colonel Thom, the guild leader. Thom and his man huddled together just off the trail. Their conversation looked to be serious.

"The colonel doesn't look happy," said Jim.

"It couldn't happen to a nicer guy," said Wyatt.

Victor leaned forward then.

"Unpleasant news, it would seem," he said.

"Unpleasant for them may be welcoming for us," said Wyatt.

Jim doubted that the one had much to do with the other.

Victor, however, thought that bad news might mean options up the road.

He would be ready.

Another of their captors stepped in front of them, tossed a food bar to each and continued on. Jim tore open his ration and took a bite. He nodded up the trail as he chewed.

"Look," he said.

Colonel Thom was giving the signal to move out. Members of his team began getting their gear together.

"Not much of a lunch break," said Wyatt, taking a bite of his food bar.

"Unpleasant or not, something clearly has him spooked," said Jim.

Ten minutes later they turned off the main trail and followed a narrow, winding path through the woods. They stopped after a few hundred yards, everyone freezing in position; everyone but those closest to Jim and his companions. They stepped hurriedly up beside their captives and gave them a cold, hard look.

Jim got the message: Make no move, make no sound.

Victor turned his head, glanced up. The guildsman beside him placed a hand on Victor's arm. Victor gave a dismissive look to the man, then looked to Jim and again to the sky.

The sound reached them then... a flyer. Very faint at first, the sound grew steadily louder. It approached, passed directly overhead and continued past. It was heading in the general direction that Jim and his captors had been traveling before they had turned off the main trail.

The sound faded away.

"One of ours," said Victor.

"A two seater," said Wyatt.

Jim looked up and down the line of his captors, noted a sense of relief visibly pass along the group. They believed they had successfully avoided a confrontation.

They started moving again. Reckoning their way forward was clear, they moved more quickly and less cautiously than before.

Another few hundred yards further, they again came to a stop, this time dropping quickly to one knee. The guildsman nearest Jim placed a firm hand on his shoulder and pushed him down.

Victor looked to Jim. *Transports,* he mouthed silently.

Jim nodded, looked overhead, above the treetops. The sound of several airships then, some distance away. The engines were larger than those of the earlier two-person flyer: deeper, more powerful.

Three ships at least. They were definitely transport craft, the fleet's smaller model: two crewmen and able to carry eight passengers.

They didn't pass directly overhead; rather they paralleled their path far to the left.

A hollow silence, then. Those around Jim rose slowly up. He was pulled to his feet and was pushed ahead as everyone started out again. They moved quickly, as quickly as before, though now Jim saw the hint of desperation; the earlier sense of confidence hadn't lasted long.

The path they were on emptied into a clearing of wild grass and tall weeds. Scattered about the clearing were five small structures half-covered in ivy and berry vines.

The guild leader pointed left and then right, sending several of the team to move into guard positions. He indicated then one of the structures. Jim and his companions were led to the building and were unceremoniously shoved inside. The door was pushed closed behind them, the base of the door dragging across the ground.

It was a single, small room, about ten feet by ten feet. The floor was bare dirt, the walls exposed roughhewn studs and old wood sheeting, some of it rotting. There were no windows, but enough light shone through wide gaps in the wall panels that they weren't totally in the dark.

Wyatt pressed a hand on the back wall and pushed. There was some give.

"As a prison cell, this shed is lacking," he said.

"This is not intended to be permanent," said Victor.

"Obviously," Wyatt growled. He gave the wall another push. There was a loud cracking sound as the wall bowed out and then back into place.

Jim lifted a foot, drawing up the anklet and chain. They wouldn't get far while bound together.

The three of them sat in a circle facing one another. Wyatt brought a short, thin wire from a hidden pocket on his belt. He quietly worked to unlock his anklet as Jim and Victor kept an eye on the door. They could hear activity outside, their captors moving about the clearing, securing the area and searching the other shacks.

Wyatt pulled apart his anklet. He rubbed his freed ankle, then shifted position and began working to free Jim. "I'll have you out in a minute."

A minute later, they heard raised voices outside: adamant, rushed. Their captors were anxious.

Something or someone struck the door. The whole building shook, dust billowing out from the walls and roof framing.

"Hurry up, Wyatt," said Jim. Whatever was happening out there, he wasn't going to be caught sitting on the floor if it came in here.

"Half a minute."

The back of the shack was half-hidden in shadow, ivy covering the wood panels that were weathered a pale gray from years of exposure. One of the panels bowed slowly out, and Jim squeezed through the opening and slipped outside. The panel closed behind him, and Jim worked his way around to the side of the building, walked cautiously along the wall to the front corner.

Peering around the corner, he saw his guildsmen abductors fighting hand-to-hand with Captain Bellamy and the ship's crew, joined now by a handful of men and women that Jim recognized as members of the Governor's Guard. Several men lay on the ground, struggling with their wounds.

A midsized transport ship passed overhead, coming down and lowering to a nearby clearing.

Someone grasped Jim's arm from behind and spun him about.

It was one of his captors.

Jim pulled free, causing him to stumble back and into the clearing. The guildsman followed after him and they struggled. Neither were armed, so they were left to using hands, fists and arms.

Jim turned sideways to his opponent, moved one leg around him and planted his foot behind him. He pushed with his shoulder and the man started to fall. He grasped at Jim's shirt, but the material slipped through his fingers and he fell backward onto the ground.

Movement beyond the fallen man caught Jim's attention. He looked up in time to see Colonel Thom, the guild leader, rushing out of the clearing. Victor was chasing after him.

Wyatt stood in front of the shack, the door behind him standing slightly ajar. He let his gaze drift slowly from left to right, taking in the activity going on about the clearing. A few of the Guild were continuing the struggle, but the fighting had for the most part ended. Ship's crewmen and members of the Governor's Guard were beginning to take guildsmen to a holding area at the far side of the clearing. A few were treating the wounded.

A young guildsman being escorted across the clearing walked past Wyatt; it was the man who had taken Wyatt's sling.

"Hold up," said Wyatt. He stepped in front of them and calmly held out his hand. The prisoner gave a sheepish grin, then lifted the sling from his belt and dropped it into Wyatt's hand. The escort tugged at the man's arm and pulled him on toward the holding area.

Wyatt noted then Colonel Thom coming back into the clearing. Victor had him by one arm, Jim held the other. The Guild team leader's clothes were torn and in disarray; it appeared there had been some confrontation between the colonel and Wyatt's friends.

Victor gave a nod to Jim, who released the colonel's arm and let Victor escort the man toward the other prisoners. Jim came over to stand beside Wyatt.

"Wyatt. I see you got your sling back."

"I was so lost without it." Jim placed a hand on his belt, his sling.

"And so you are found again." Jim looked about the clearing. He started hesitantly, "Was anyone..."

"Killed?" Wyatt shrugged. "I can't say. I just got here myself." Wyatt watched as one of the wounded was helped to the prisoner holding area. "But it doesn't look like it."

"I would hate to think I was cause of... you know."

"I know." Wyatt gave a slow nod. "I think we're good."

Victor and Captain Bellamy started across the clearing toward Jim and Wyatt. Behind them, Commander Thornton of the Governor's Guard began directing his team to escort the prisoners from the holding area and to the trailhead and the path leading to the nearby clearing where transport shuttles waited.

"Is everyone all right?" asked Captain Bellamy.

"We're fine, Captain," said Jim. "I was about to ask you the same question."

"Minor injuries, only. Not to worry, Jim."

"Thank you, Captain."

"You are quite welcome." Bellamy looked to Wyatt, to Victor, back to Jim. "The Governor's shuttle is on its way. We'll have the three of you home in a few hours."

Chapter Ten

The long, sleek air shuttle hovered above the tarmac, descended slowly then to one of the open landing pads. The support aircraft that had accompanied the governor's shuttle circled the airfield.

The governor's shuttle was a simple design, though roomier than the other airships in the small fleet. The governor rarely used it himself, but accepted that it was often required when he traveled. He didn't want to make the Guard's responsibility for his safety any more difficult than necessary.

In this instance, it was carrying his son and Jim's companions safely home.

The shuttle settled onto the landing pad. This pad was in the heart of the tarmac, an expansive airfield located just outside the Capital grounds. The field consisted of several dozen landing pads of various sizes, most of which were currently occupied.

On the pad, with engines winding down, the ramp extended and the door slid aside. Jim came down the ramp, Victor and Wyatt following after. They had cleaned up en route and were wearing fresh clothes.

An open-air cart pulled up to the foot of the ramp. Jim and his friends climbed aboard and the driver steered the cart away from the shuttle and toward one of the airfield gates. They traveled the quarter mile to the governor's estate in relative silence, the only sound the dull hum of the cart's electric motor.

The driver brought the cart to a stop in front of the main archway into the capital grounds. Two members of the Governor's Guard were waiting for them. Jim, Victor and Wyatt were escorted on foot into the plaza.

The plaza was winding walkways, raised garden beds, flowerbeds, groomed bushes and trees, all enclosed by stately buildings. Most of the buildings were administrative, though there was also a museum, a library, and several apartment complexes.

Wyatt left his friends midway across the plaza, turning onto a sidewalk that would take him to one of those apartment buildings. Jim and Victor continued on to the governor's mansion, their escort following several paces behind.

The mansion was an unassuming structure with three wings and a central hub. The governor's office and those of his staff made up one wing. A second wing held governing support departments, while living quarters made up the third wing.

The mansion's front hall had a high ceiling, lamps hanging on the walls and sitting on side tables. Large arches opened to hallways leading to each of the three wings.

Victor left Jim here, heading into the living quarters wing. Much of the wing consisted of the governor's family residence, but there were also a handful of small apartments, including Victor's.

One of the escort stepped forward and indicated Jim should follow him into the support wing. He led Jim along the wide, well-lit hallway. Wide doors were set far apart, each with a brass plaque designating the support department beyond the door.

There was a smaller, nondescript door at the end of the hall. The escort opened the door and stepped aside. Jim passed through and the escort closed the door, waiting outside.

Jim entered a small library. Walls were lined with shelves filled with books. The wall opposite the only door had two tall, narrow windows. There were several comfortable chairs with side tables and pole lamps. There was a heavy wooden table with four wood chairs in the center of the room.

Jim's father was sitting in one of the easy chairs, beneath the soft glow of the pole lamp beside him. The governor set the book that he had been reading on the side table and stood. He smiled and his face lit up.

"Jim, my son," he said.

"Hello, father," said Jim. He reached his father and they hugged. It was several moments before the governor was willing to let go. Even when he stepped back he continued to hold onto Jim's shoulders.

"You look well, Jim," he said. "Are you well?"

"I'm fine."

"You're sure?" The governor released Jim's shoulders, placed a hand on his back and guided him to the table. They sat.

Jim knew that his father would have received a complete report while Jim and his friends were en route to the capital. He also knew that a report would have done only so much to ease his father's mind.

He reassured his father. It had been a unique experience, multiple experiences, actually, and he had come through it just fine. As had Victor and Wyatt.

His mother had been extremely upset, had been pleased and relieved to hear of Jim's rescue. The governor told Jim that his mother was in the family residence overseeing the preparations for quite the welcome home celebration.

The door to the library opened and Mrs. Weatherly, the governor's administrative assistant, took one step into the room and waited, a folder in hand.

"Come, come," said the governor, waving a hand for her to approach.

"Sorry to interrupt, governor."

"Not at all, Mrs. Weatherly." The governor took the folder. "Thank you."

Mrs. Weatherly nodded, stepped back and looked to Jim. She smiled.

"Welcome home, James."

No one but Mrs. Weatherly called him *'James'*.

"Thank you, Mrs. Weatherly."

Mrs. Weatherly left the library, closing the door behind her.

"One moment, Jim," said the governor, opening the folder.

Jim watched as his father read through the documentation. It was one or two minutes before he closed the folder and set it on the table.

"Well," he stated flatly.

"Sir?"

The governor frowned as he glowered at the closed folder.

"A preliminary report on the interrogations of your captors."

"The Founders Guild."

"The Guild. Yes." The governor's frown deepened. "They knew their actions would cost them much."

"They were going to turn me over to the pirates."

"So it would seem," said the governor. "They do have a tenuous relationship with the Silver Pirates, and this might have strengthened those ties. But to sacrifice their truce with us... and more, the retribution they knew would come. I do not understand."

"They must have been offered a lot."

"The pirates are closely allied to the slavers, and the slavers are most unhappy with you."

"Good," said Jim. "I am particularly honored by the bounty they offer."

Jim had been working to bring down the slavers ever since his experiences on ShadowWorld several years earlier. He had used his father's network throughout the Frontier Worlds and the Outlands since then to disrupt the slave industry. Success had been sporadic, failures frequent, but as Jim gained experience so did the slavers' frustrations.

And with each year that passed, Jim's credibility grew. World leaders had grown to respect this young son of the governor.

For now, Jim operated in an unofficial capacity under the mentorship of his proud father. That status would change once he came of age, when he would accept an official role in Frontier Worlds government.

The governor slid his chair back and stood up. He placed a hand on his son's shoulder.

"Come, Jim. I am sure your mother has completed homecoming preparations."

end